This Book

Belongs To:

_____

_____

First published 2018 © Twinkl Ltd of Wards Exchange,
197 Ecclesall Road, Sheffield S11 8HW

ISBN: 978-1-914331-35-0

Copyright © Twinkl Ltd. 2021

MIX
Paper from
responsible sources
FSC® C013056

We're passionate about giving our children a sustainable future, which is why
this book is made from Forest Stewardship Council® certified paper.
Learn how our Twinkl Green policy gives the planet a helping hand at
www.twinkl.com/twinkl-green.

Printed in the United Kingdom.

10 9 8 7 6 5 4 3 2 1

A catalogue record for this book is available from the British Library.

A TWINKL ORIGINAL

Rainforest Calling

Twinkl Educational Publishing

Monday 24th March (The Emergent Layer)

Tuesday 25th March (The Canopy)

Wednesday 26th March (The Understorey)

Thursday 27th march (The Forest Floor)

Friday 28th march (Forest Floor/understorey/Canopy)

name:	Daisy Field
class:	4JC
Rainforest Journal	

9:50 a.m.

I wonder if the person who gave the rainforest its name had ever actually been there. Surely, if they had, they'd have called it the 'plant forest' instead.

Mrs Curtis, my teacher, told us that more than two thirds of the world's plant species live in rainforest environments . That's more than 80,000 different plants!

There's no way that I'm telling my Grandma Wilkins THAT! She'd be on the first plane to Brazil with her lucky gardening gloves because she really LOVES plants. Do you know, she once told me that she might love plants even more than she loves my mum! Don't worry, I haven't told my mum that.

That's one of the reasons why I volunteered for this project — so that I could tell my grandma about all the plants. Mrs Curtis wanted one of us to spend a whole week looking at some webcams in the Amazonian rainforest.

I put my hand straight up. My best friend, Millie, said that the last time she'd seen anything move as fast as my arm was when someone told her daft brother that the bank was giving away free money. Who WOULDN'T volunteer to spend the whole week looking at the Amazon? I think that I'd be really good at spotting all the different plants and animals.

As soon as Mrs Curtis looked at me, I knew that I hadn't been picked. She had the same expression on her face that she uses to tell us that we've got a maths question wrong as she said, "Maybe next time, Daisy." Jack Walters got picked instead, but he changed his mind when he found out that we're only allowed to look at the webcams during our breaks and at lunchtime. He said that there was no way that he was going to miss playing football in the playground. So Mrs Curtis ended up choosing me anyway! I don't mind having to do normal lessons — I got nine out of ten on my spellings last week. Still can't spell rhinnosoraus, though.

Mrs Curtis said that I have to write a journal entry to tell the rest of the class what I've seen on the webcams. I haven't written a journal before. The only things I write at home are lists of my favourite songs and the things I want for Christmas, but mrs Curtis said not to worry and to just write as I like to speak. I think that should make it easier!

A 'green conversation' charity set the webcams up a few years ago (I'm not actually sure what a green conversation is, or a red or yellow or pink conversation either) and when mrs Curtis logged on with her laptop, she showed me that we can move the webcams with the arrows on the keyboard. If I want to move left or right, up or down, I just press the arrows. I can even move from camera to camera so that I can explore each layer of the rainforest! mrs Curtis also said that the Amazon rainforest is over 5,000 miles away from our school, yet I can still move the lens in any direction I want. Sometimes, technology is amazing!

I'd love to spend all my time looking for the monkeys, or even a Bigfoot! my dad says scientists think that there are still over five million animal species waiting to be discovered in the world and most of those probably live in the rainforest. He wants me to keep my eyes peeled for a Bigfoot. He says, "Daisy, that'll be like winning the lottery!"

My dad thinks that he knows lots about the rainforest. I think that he might have read the same books as Mrs Curtis because they both said that lots of what we all take for granted comes from the rainforest. Those beans that people use to make chocolate come from there, and pineapples, too, plus the ginger that goes into yummy biscuits... even rubber for the soles of my trainers.

Millie says that her uncle has an important job at the city museum and HE reckons that more than twenty-five percent (that's a quarter) of all medicines use plants from the rainforest. So if you stay up too late and have a headache, or get an iffy tummy after you've eaten one of your dad's home-made curries, the medicine that you are given could be made from rainforest plants. How amazing is that?

What I'd really like to find, though, is a new kind of flower — maybe one of those beautiful orchids. When you find something new like that, those clever people you see on the documentary channels sometimes let you name them. I'd call mine the Wilkins orchid, after Grandma Wilkins. That would make her feel very important, and she tells me that she's always wanted to be a VIP!

10:41 a.m.
Mrs Curtis wants me to visit one of the four layers of the rainforest each day so, because it's Monday today, I'll log onto the conservation charity's webcam in the emergent layer during lunchtime break. That's the top part of the rainforest, where you can see all the clouds that are formed when water vapour rises from the forest. (By the way, I realised that it's not a con-vers-ation charity at all — it's a con-serv-ation charity. Silly me! No wonder Mrs Curtis has circled it.)

Tomorrow, I'll check out the canopy layer. I can't wait for that because the charity website says that's where most of the orchids are. Howler monkeys live there, too, so imagine if I saw or heard one of those! Jack Walters says that a howler monkey's cry is so loud, it can be heard over five kilometres away. He makes things up, though, so I take everything he says with a pinch of salt.

After that, I'll look at the understorey and then, on Thursday, I'll explore the forest floor. Mrs Curtis has said that on Friday, I can look at whatever I want, so that's when I'll look for an orchid — and maybe Dad's Bigfoot, too.

I have to keep notes about what I see. That's why I'm writing these journal entries. These are going to be my 'observations' and then I've got to share the highlights in a talk to the whole class next week. (I asked my mum what highlights are, but she said that the only highlights she knows about are the blonde ones that she puts in my Auntie Tanya's hair every month.)

Anyway, Mrs Curtis said that if my rainforest talk is REALLY good, she'll ask our headteacher, Ms Smeaton, if I can present it in assembly. Ms Smeaton gives out badges to children who take

part in assemblies and I've always wanted one of
those! millie will be so jealous.

OK, that's it for now. we've got another spelling
test in five minutes. I hope that mrs curtis doesn't
ask me to spell hippipotamoose.

12:41 p.m.
How am I supposed to know how to spell
eggsajerate? I can't even say it properly, never
mind write it.

Still, eight out of ten is way better than Jack
Walters. He only got six of his words right and
mrs curtis told him that he should definitely
know how to spell DISASTROUS after his penalty
miss in that football semi-final last week. (mrs
curtis thinks that Jack might have lost his sense
of humour at the same time as the team lost
that match.) It's lunchtime now and Jack is in
the playground, sulking. I bet he wishes that
he hadn't turned down the chance to use the
rainforest webcams now – they're amazing!

I've just finished looking at the emergent layer.
It's even higher than that huge ride I went on
with millie in Blackpool last summer. Last week,

Mrs Curtis told us that the treetops in the emergent layer can be over 70 metres high. Dad says that's over two hundred feet — but what if the person measuring it has really small feet, or huge ones? I don't really understand Dad's old-fashioned measurements.

Anyway, it was really high up and I felt dizzy, even though I never left my chair. The camera must have been strapped to one of those massive Brazil nut trees. They're the highest trees in the forest and I had a view across the entire canopy. It's so incredible to see a place that hasn't been changed by humans — Mrs Curtis says that the area I'm looking at is a protected part of the forest and there is no trace of humans for miles and miles. Parts of the forest like these are protected so that no one touches them and they stay as perfectly natural environments for the plants and animals underneath the trees.

I've found out that there are rainforests all over the world and that these webcams are in the Brazilian part of the Amazon rainforest. The Amazon is the biggest rainforest in the world and actually stretches into nine countries. NINE! As well as Brazil, there's also Peru, Colombia, Venezuela, Ecuador, Bolivia, Guyana, Suriname and French Guiana. That's a lot of countries.

I read somewhere that the Amazon rainforest stretches for more than FIVE MILLION square kilometres. That's a lot of kilometres, but why are they square? What's wrong with round kilometres, or even triangle-shaped ones? I'll have to ask mrs Curtis about that.

What's even more mind-blowing is the fact that the rainforest used to be even bigger! Bloggers have chopped down three quarters of a million kilometres in just forty years. No, wait — it's loggers, not bloggers. Those loggers chop down the trees and sell the wood. Then, instead of planting more trees, they just dig up the land for growing crops or farming cattle. I think that's called DEFORESTATION.

There's a page on the charity's website (they have a LOT of web pages) which talks about how the local people make money and get jobs, and how logging is important for the local economy...

The wood harvested through the forestry industry in South America can be <u>exported</u> as:

- pulp
- raw wood
- wood chips
- laminated wood & flooring
- paper
- furniture
- frames
- packaging

These products are sent all over the world and generate a lot of money for the countries of South America.

I think that's something to do with money.

Do you know what's really strange? The charity's first camera is so high up that the treetops didn't look like they belonged to a forest at all. It's really windy up there and the thick branches and leaves sway and ripple like waves in a huge, green sea. I wonder if the parrots and monkeys sometimes feel more like fish...

It's really wet up there, too, which you'd expect from a rainforest, I suppose. Clouds hang so close to the treetops that it feels like you could reach out and grab a handful of fluffiness. The wind whooshes them past so fast that sometimes, it's more like watching giant sheep racing each other.

At school, we learnt about the water cycle. Mrs Curtis says that water vapour condenses when it gets cooler — this is how we get rain. The hot forest makes the water vapour rise, and the cool river air makes it fall down again as rain. It's so simple and yet so clever!

I liked it best when the sun shone through the clouds. The leaves all seem to be coated in some kind of wax. It looks like somebody has slapped on some of that suntan oil that my Auntie Sonya uses out in the garden, so I wonder if it helps to protect the leaves from the strong sun, too. They look so slippery, I reckon that the insects could probably use them as skating rinks. When they caught the sunlight, they glistened even brighter than Grandma Wilkins' opal earrings. I should have brought my sunglasses.

I saw some amazing blue birds. I remember seeing a photo on the charity's website and it said that they were called cotingas. I spotted parrots, too — macaws, I think. They were all perched in the treetops and if you didn't know that they were birds, you'd easily think that the clouds had been raining multicoloured paint.

Mrs Curtis likes howler monkeys but I didn't see any of those. I'm sure that I heard one, though. The webcam picks up rainforest noises and that monkey makes what my grandad would call a 'right racket'! The poor things sound like they're gargling with rusty nails. And they're so LOUD! In fact, the only person I know who can shout as loud as a howler monkey is Mr Paterson, our caretaker. Now, he'd give them a proper run for their money!

12:52 p.m.
Mrs Curtis told me that I have to make a separate journal entry every time I leave the webcam and then log back on. I asked her if that meant even when I pop to the bathroom and she said yes. I only went for some tissue to blow my nose with but she said that I had to write my journals as if I were a real scientist, and that means accurately recording my time.

I love playing around with the webcam. I found out that I can use the scroll wheel on the mouse to zoom in as well. So I zoomed in A LOT! I'm glad I did, too, because among the trillions of tropical leaves, I found some really beautiful orchids. I can see why Grandma Wilkins likes orchids as much as she does. They're so colourful and the petals have amazing patterns, like a kaleidoscope!

Orchids really like it up in the emergent layer because there's so much sunshine. Grandma says that some have roots that don't even need soil – they can actually drink moisture from the air. I never realised that plants could be so clever!

Oh, I nearly forgot! I also saw something a bit strange. It was a bird, but not one of the parrots.

I didn't see it at first – it was really well disguised and I thought it was just a broken tree branch. In fact, it was only when it opened its big yellow goggle-eyes that I spotted it and I had to zoom in to get a good view. Poor thing – it's really ugly and sort of like a cross between a tawny owl (the ones with the nice brown and white feathers) and a car with big headlamps. Its eyes are so HUGE that it looks startled all the time – as if one of the other animals has just jumped out from behind a big leaf and shouted BOO! Oh, and the poor thing's little thin beak looks squashed, as if it's been caught in a set of lift doors.

I bet it's really jealous of the parrots because its feathers aren't colourful at all. But what makes this funny thing seem really odd is its mouth. I'd say it belongs on a frog, not a bird, and it seems to be permanently turned down into a sad frown. You should see it when it opens its beak though – that funny bird's mouth is almost wider than its entire face.

The Internet is great for finding out about stuff, so I did an image search and found out that the bird is actually called a POTOO. Now, I understand why I didn't see it at first – it's really good at hiding. What's unusual about the potoo on my screen is its markings: the darker feathers on its chest make a sort of lopsided heart shape.

These birds normally only come out at night. Maybe that's why its goggle-eyes are so big – so it can see in the dark. I wonder why it was still awake... maybe it's scared, or looking for something. Or perhaps it stayed up past its bedtime to talk to one of those colourful macaws.

Actually, one of the birds with the bright tail feathers seemed to be arguing with the potoo. The macaw was yakking and squawking away and the potoo was answering back. They were making a real din!

Potoos (Nyctibiidae) are sometimes called poor-me-ones because of their haunting call. Potoos are nocturnal and eat mainly insects. During the day, they perch upright on the stumps of tree branches and lay their spotted eggs directly onto the trees. The birds' remarkable camouflage allows them to look like part of the tree stumps.

It's funny because you'd hope that a bird with such quirky looks would have a great singing voice (like a lovely robin or a nightingale) but it definitely doesn't. In fact, it was more of a wail than a chirp. It's a good job that there are no mirrors in the rainforest, because then it really would have a reason to feel sorry for itself.

I probably won't see that poor potoo again. I'm visiting the canopy layer tomorrow and, if I'm really lucky, I might get to see a sloth. Everyone loves sloths!

Daisy's Emergent Checklist

- [x] macaws
- [x] Cotingas
- [x] Capuchin monkeys
- [ ] New type of orchid
- [x] Potoo

"Hey, Rodrigo, my feathered friend! I think that this strange one-eye thing might be looking at you. Come and see!"

Me and my big, silly beak! A clever potoo like me should have known better – Rodrigo is a macaw, and no one in the whole forest likes being looked at more than macaws do. Show-offs.

You see, one-eye, my colourful friend doesn't care that you are clinging to our trees and staring at us – Rodrigo just thinks it's another reason for him to pose and show off his bright feathers. Trust me, one-eye, he certainly does not need **another** reason.

"Do you think they like my feathers, Pedro?" he squawks. "Which do you think they like best, eh? Yellow? Or maybe blue?"

Sometimes, I think that Rodrigo loves himself way, **way** too much. "Rodrigo, nobody is impressed by your feathers – lots of birds around here have colourful feathers. The whole forest has already seen your bottom far too many times, OK?"

Take my word for it, my new one-eyed compadre, no potoo wants to see a macaw's booty shaking like that, especially after a breakfast feast of grubs and beetles. It's like watching a wonky rainbow wobbling in a storm, and makes my tummy roll like I've just flapped from the top of the tallest tree to the forest floor. But this potoo will keep his beak shut – those flashy macaws can be so sensitive.

It's just that this forest is full of many things that are so much more beautiful than Rodrigo's feathers. Look at all these leaves and flower petals below us. Do you notice how they shine, and how the raindrops sparkle in the sunlight? Aren't they a delight?

What about the swirly swarms of butterflies under the canopy? They do make tasty snacks, but I like to admire the way they flutter and fly, too. Food that looks as good as it tastes – what can be better than that, huh? Just wait until you go beneath the leaves, one-eye. That's when you'll see those colourful creatures fluttering by, like tiny fragments of a broken rainbow. Every week, I see new colours and patterns.

I wonder what kind of creature you are: a strange new forest animal, perhaps, or a brand new kind of plant... I'm not sure. You're green like the bushes and trees but look at your skin: it's hard and tough like a caiman's tail, and smooth, too, just like a turtle's belly. I am one puzzled potoo because you don't have any legs or wings or even a beak, and I haven't seen you walk or crawl or fly yet. In fact, all you ever do is sit there on a tree like a lazy, sleeping sloth – just not nearly as pretty, huh?

Hello?

Has the jaguar got your tongue? Do you even

know that I'm here? You're not even looking at me, one-eye. All you do is look this way, then the other way.

Hello?

Wait! Of course! I know why you can't see me. How foolish of me – I am Pedro the potoo! And potoos are **masters of disguise**.

It's true! Clever birds like Pedro can vanish from view in one flap of a hummingbird's wing, or sit in the same place for hours without **ever** being seen. I'd like to see one of those flashy 'look-at-me' macaws try to do that, huh? Let's face it, you could see Rodrigo with your eyes closed – and in this forest, if you're easy to see, you're an easy-to-catch meal for those sharp-toothed predators.

Rodrigo lives up here in the tops of the tallest trees, where it's windy and wet and there are fewer hungry predators – comprende? Macaws don't like being reminded that they're scaredy-birds, though. So Rodrigo tells me that he stays up here **only** because he can crack the Brazil nuts with his beak and gobble them with his special tongue. (Typical. Macaws like him think that everything about them is special.)

Personally, I think that it's far too wet and windy up here for a little bird like me to fly. It's dazzlingly hot, too – probably because there's nothing above us to hide us from the sun up here in the tallest trees.

Trees! Of course, that's why you're here – to look at all the wonderful, magnificent forest trees. Aren't they amazing? They seem to stretch on forever, following our beautiful river as far as the eye can see. You can't have a forest without trees – without trees, where would birds like me sleep? Where could I perch, out of reach of the nasties creeping around the forest floor? Where would Rodrigo get his tasty nuts from? And where would **you** be, one-eye?

Hey, do you want to know what has been ruffling my feathers lately? Something dreadful is happening to our beautiful trees...

They're vanishing!

My forest friends and I think that there are some

nasty tree-stealers prowling the forest. Have you seen them, one-eye? One minute, a potoo can be hopping from branch to branch, enjoying the dark and the quiet between the trees; the next, he's blinded by blazing sunlight and deafened by more noise than a troop of angry howler monkeys. It's true! Every day, more of our trees disappear. You don't think that those tree-stealers want to take the **entire** forest, do you?

Rodrigo sometimes says that he thinks that those tree-stealers might not like us birds.

"No more trees means no more birds," he yaks. "We all have to fly away!"

That's crazy talk, right? But my friends and I are scared, one-eye – so scared that birds like Rodrigo have been talking to those fly-away birds (you know, the ones who come here for holidays when it's not so wet). Rodrigo says that he could fly away with them to a new home, far away from our lovely forest.

"Rodrigo can save the macaws, Pedro," he promises. "Rodrigo will lead them somewhere new, where there's no chop-chopping and everybody is safe."

"But why would anyone want to leave a forest this beautiful?" I ask him. "We have everything we need right here, like fruits and nuts and berries to eat, drinking water that falls from the clouds, plus thick, waxy leaves for the birds and monkeys and lizards to shelter beneath. It's the perfect place!"

Even the forest plants are good to us, one-eye. Many make us well when we're ill or injured. Last summer, I rubbed my poorly wing on a sprig of cordoncillo leaves and it stopped hurting in just a few quick flaps.

I have so many friends here, too. Why would I want to say goodbye to Alice the agouti, or my favourite sloth, Tolle, and even squeezy Winfrey the tree boa? I think that I might even miss Francisco the falcon, at least when he's not trying to gobble potoos for his lunch, eh? We're all really happy here.

I just wish that I could convince Rodrigo to stay. He usually groans and says things like, "What's the use in being here if there are no more trees?

It's better to fly away and find a new home to love, Pedro – maybe on a mountain or an island."

Yesterday, I tried to tell him **again** that an island is no good for animals like the sloth, the agouti or the snake. They don't have wings – how will they get to this new home?

"What's your bright idea, then?" he asked. "How will Pedro the potoo save this forest?"

That's when I tapped my beak and told that noisy macaw all about C.A.R.E.

"Care?"

"Not 'care'," I told him. "**C.A.R.E.!**"

I think that Rodrigo's bird brain might be too small to understand, even though I explained to him (really slowly) that C.A.R.E. is 'Creatures Against Rainforest Evacuation'.

He just looked back at me as if he thought that my egg might have fallen out of the nest before I hatched.

"Rodrigo, we have to make a stand," I told him. "We have to stay and show those nasty tree-stealers that this is our home, comprende? They can't just come here to chop and chop. No trees means no world."

I think that I might have frightened him because that's when Rodrigo started to shake. "No world!" he shrieked, flapping and squawking as if lightning had nipped at his bottom. "No world!"

I think that Rodrigo is too scared to listen any more. But, hey, perhaps if Pedro spent a little time showing **you** how everyone needs the forest, you might want to listen and help, eh?

My friends tell me that they've seen one-eyes in different places: down below in the canopy and on the forest floor... in fact, they've spotted you in every layer of our beautiful forest. So I'll come looking for you and we can explore the forest together, OK?

Great! Fantastic! Amazing! That's what we'll do. It's a plan! We'll team up and Pedro will introduce you to his wonderful home. Because we C.A.R.E.

Right?

29

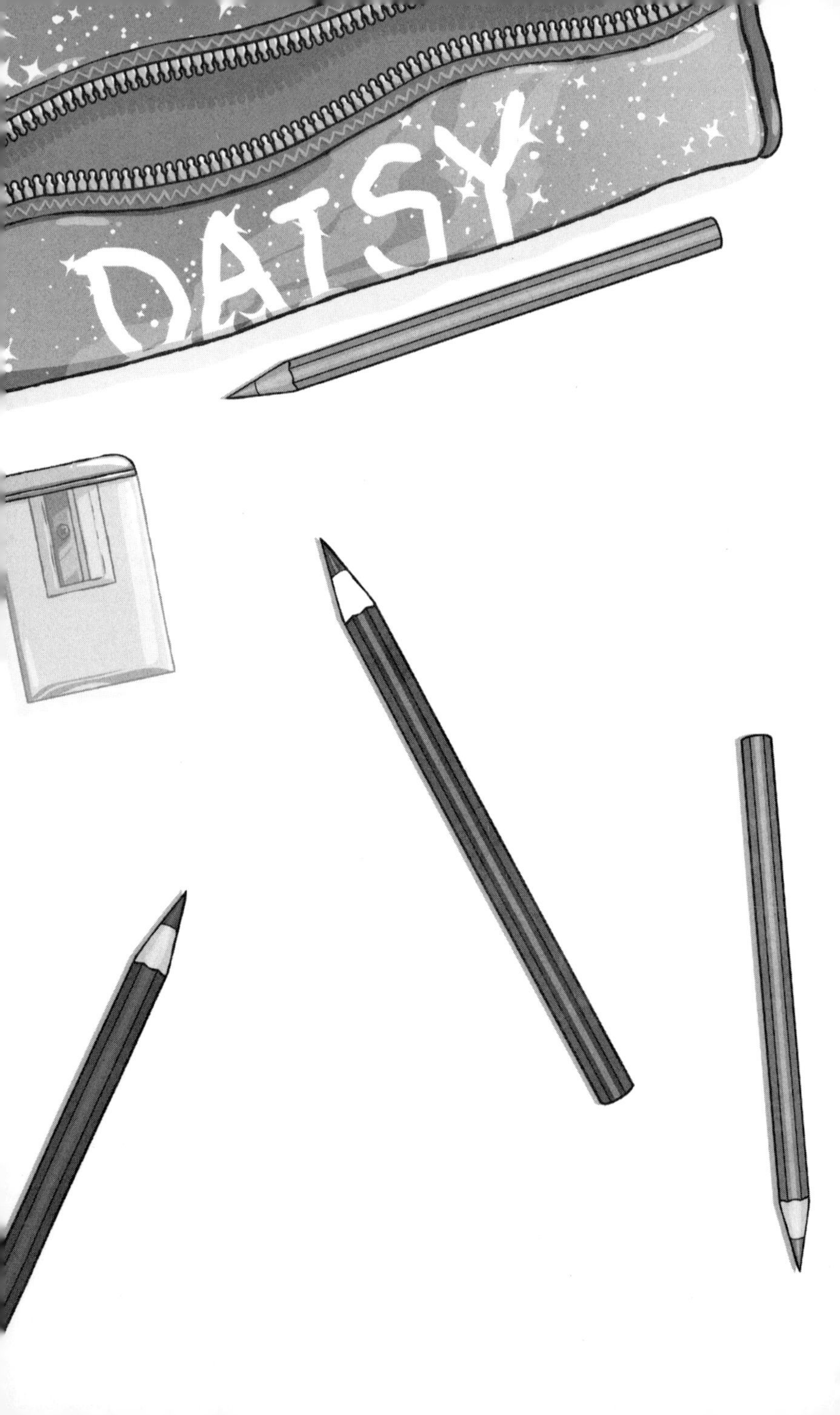
DAISY

name:	Daisy Field
class:	4JC
Rainforest Journal	

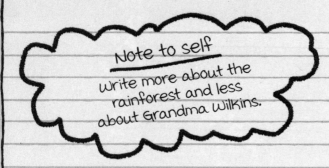

Note to self
Write more about the
rainforest and less
about Grandma Wilkins.

Tuesday 25ᵗʰ March

There are lots of different trees in the canopy.
The leaves are all green but there are many
different shades and I've seen lots of shapes, too.

Some are long and narrow, with that waxy
surface and a channel running right down the
middle. Raindrops roll down the channels like
tumbling diamonds, helping the rain to get right
to the roots of the trees. Others are really broad
and remind me of huge dinner plates. Some of
these seem to be homes for little insects and
even brightly coloured frogs. I think the leaves
are that big so that they can catch the sunlight —
my teacher says that trees like sunlight. I wonder
if that's why Dad's new solar panels are so big,
too.

There are so many trees in the canopy that
the branches all weave together like knotted
shoelaces. With all those big, thick leaves woven

around each other, not all the sunlight gets through so it's a bit darker than the emergent layer above.

The **canopy** can also be referred to as the habitat zone or upper layer.

The canopy layer is also known as the 'habitat zone'. That's because lots more animals and insects live in the canopy than in any other layer. I think it helps that they have lots of branches to walk along and that the trees provide shelter and safety.

I've prepared a checklist of animals that I'd like to study in each layer. For the canopy, this includes toucans, monkeys, lizards and sloths, but I haven't seen any of these yet. I've been mainly focusing on the vegetation. During my next visit to the rainforest, I'll try to find some animals to watch.

Dear Ms Smeaton,

I hope this journal entry is better than yesterday's. Mrs Curtis has told me to concentrate more on what I see in the rainforest and not what my grandma likes.

33

<u>12:23 p.m.</u>

This afternoon, I'm going to be exploring the canopy again. I can see why it's called 'the habitat zone' – it's amazing!

Do you remember how I said earlier that it's a little darker in this layer? Well, I think that's because there are so many trees growing tightly beside each other. All the leaves and branches knit together like one giant blanket, covering everything.

...ing up just under ...all the world's forests.

Tropical rainforests receive around 12 hours of sunlight a day. Most of this is concentrated on the canopy cover, giving the forest a temperature of 21 to 30 degrees Celsius. The environment maintains a humidity of 77% to 88% all year round.

Deforestation

The canopy traps the heat and makes it humid, like the inside of my grandad's greenhouse in summer. That probably explains why there are so many plants here. You should see them! They're beautiful – so bright and colourful, in so many shapes and sizes. Some plants even grow on top of each other. I think these might be the EPIPHYTES that I've read about. They get their water and nutrients from the air and rainwater, so there's no need for them to grow on the ground. You can actually find plants growing quite happily, just sitting on a tree branch!

My favourite plants are the ones that look like the heads of purple lions, with petals that spread out like a great big, wiggly mane. I also love those orange ones that look just like colourful, spiky pine cones on stalks.

You really won't believe this, but the rainforest is full of caniverus plants, too. It's true! There's this one plant that looks like a little upturned trumpet with sweet nectar around the edge. It waits and waits and waits until a fly or an insect or maybe even a frog sits on the edge to get the nectar. The surface is slippery so the poor creatures that land on it topple straight down into the open mouth bit. The creatures have no chance of getting out, either, because the long trumpet acts like the plant's stomach and actually digests the creatures that fall in there.

I wish that I'd been able to spend more time exploring the canopy. It's so busy and loud! The whole place is bustling with birds and monkeys. I love those monkeys. They're hard to see because there are so many leaves and branches but, once I had spotted them, I couldn't take my eyes off them. They race in groups along the branches, screeching and squabbling as they snatch fruit from the trees. I'm sure that some of them think

that they can actually fly, because they just leap
off the trees onto the massive leaves and
spindly branches, sometimes metres below.
I'd be WAY too scared to do that!

There are even more birds than monkeys. Some
are tiny, like the hummingbirds that hover in
front of flowers and dip their beaks into the
nectar. But others are HUGE. I think that I
saw an eagle perched on a branch, but
I'm not sure. It was the parrots and
parakeets that I really liked. They're
everywhere, flapping around on the
branches like squawking gangs, and they
seem to come in all kinds of colours, too. The little
ones beat their wings almost too fast to see.

I couldn't live in the canopy. It's way too noisy
and the sound of all those birds and monkeys
together almost gave me a headache. I'm sure I
could hear a woodpecker tap-tapping on a tree
nearby. I wonder if they're taking part in some
kind of rainforest talent competition, to see which
species can make the loudest racket. Every time
a monkey shrieks, a bird squawks back even
louder and that sets the rest of them off, until
the whole forest sounds like it's filled with hordes

of angry football supporters.

12:46 p.m.
I've started another new journal entry because I had to nip back to class to get my water bottle. Exploring the rainforest is thirsty work!

When I got back, I moved the webcam with the arrow keys and I came across a group of toucans on one platform — they have huge, yellow beaks that look as if they've been dipped in black ink. I definitely saw a lizard, too. It was eating some kind of long-legged insect — maybe a spider.

The rainforest is no place to be if you don't like spiders. I read that there are more than 3,000 different types living there. Some of them love jumping and can leap from tree to tree. Others are as big as a saucer and actually catch and eat birds! But even those are not as scary as the Brazilian wandering spider. That's one of the most poisonous spiders in the world and I definitely wouldn't want to bump into one of those!

The spiders in the genus can grow to have a leg span of 13 to 15 cm. The **Brazilian wandering spider** wanders across the jungle floor instead of living in a lair or spinning a web. While some other araneomorph spiders have a longer leg span.

I still can't believe how big some of the leaves are. Do you know that monkeys and birds can actually sit on them? I explained to our caretaker, mr Paterson, that it's so the leaves can soak up as much sunlight as possible.

mr Paterson's really nosy! He was supposed to be fixing the chair next to mine but he said that my work was much more interesting than his, so he stopped to watch me explore. He says that he wants to go to the rainforest when he retires, to see all the animals. He says that he wants to go to Benidorm, too, but the only creatures that he expects to find there are party animals!

He wanted me to zoom in and find a capuchin monkey. I saw some up in the emergent layer but they probably live a bit higher up than this camera is. Luckily, mr Paterson loves sloths just as much and he gave me a high five when we found one asleep on a branch. At least, I think it was asleep — it must have been there a long time, too, because it actually had moss growing on its fur!

I didn't know that sloths were so cute — or that they had long claws like a bear's. They don't use them for fighting, though. mr Paterson said that they're just for climbing and gripping onto trees, and sometimes for scaring away predators. I'd certainly be scared by claws like that.

I wonder if our caretaker went to universe city, because he knows a lot about the rainforest. He even told me about the illegal loggers. These are the naughty groups who chop down the trees without permission — like Jack Walters, when he goes to the toilet without putting his hand up and asking mrs Curtis first. Jack says that he has to do it, otherwise he'll have an accident.

mr Paterson says that it's the same for the illegal loggers — they have to do it, too! Only, they need to chop the trees down for money. It's the only job that they can get and the only way to earn enough to feed and clothe themselves and their families.

Lots of people want them to stop. The rainforest trees help to keep the planet healthy. I read that they soak up tons of carbon dioxide so that the rest of us can breathe safely — so if we chop them down, what happens to us all then?

Also, the conservation charity says that only one percent of all the rainforest plants have been properly studied. Think what we might find in the other ninety-nine percent. What if there are plants that can help our doctors cure flu, or special leaves that could stop the arthritis in my grandma's fingers from hurting her so much when she's gardening? How incredible would that be?!

I don't know what to think about that. The charity website says:

Illegal logging is helping to destroy the rainforest and kills lots of the animals and plants that live there.

Illegal logging in the rainforest facts:

But really, those people are just going to work like my mum and dad, so that children like me can have new shoes and food and toys. Maybe I'll ask Mrs Curtis which is more important – trees or people.

Oh, guess what! I saw that funny bird again – the potoo! You'll think that I'm crazy because the rainforest is enormous, but I know that it was the same one as before because it had that heart shape on its chest. It does look very much like a tree stump when it stays still – it's really clever but I spotted its yellow googly eyes, like a couple of bulging egg yolks.

This can't just be a coincidence because the rainforest is so incredibly big and this is a totally different camera, so what are the chances of the same potoo finding it? Part of me wonders if that bird actually came looking for the camera... but that's silly, isn't it?

I wish that mr Paterson had stuck around to watch the potoo with me so that he might have seen how strangely it started to behave. Do you know, I'm sure that it wanted me to follow it along the tree branches. I had to tap the cursor keys really quickly to keep up but then it just stopped and stared out into space. I don't know what it was looking at because there was nothing there — not even any trees. It was just a gap in the forest about the size of a football pitch. Sunlight flooded the clearing but the bird didn't seem happy. It was flapping its wings like a demented conductor, and hopping up and down on the branch so hard that I thought it might snap. It wailed and wailed so much that I had to turn down the volume. The poor thing — I don't know what was wrong with it!

I wonder if I should mention the potoo to Mrs Curtis. It seems a bit funny that it was there again today. If I was as daft as Jack Walters, I might start to think that IT was actually watching me.

Daisy's Canopy Checklist

- [x] Toucans
- [x] Monkeys
- [x] Lizards
- [ ] Harpy Eagles
- [x] Sloth
- [ ] New type of orchid
- [x] Potoo

Hey, you're back. Wonderful! Great! I bet you couldn't keep away, huh? Trust me, Pedro senses these things.

Right now, I'm feeling that you and I have a lot in common. We both like sitting in trees, don't we? You've picked a wonderful spot to soak up all these views of the forest. I really couldn't have chosen a better perch myself.

Up here in the canopy is where your new friend Pedro the potoo lives. Sure, I visit other parts of the forest to see my friends, but here is where I hatched and here is where I can easily find food and shelter.

Look over there, one-eye. Notice how those twisting branches twirl and coil around each other? They make me think of two long-lost snakes hugging after years apart. Don't you agree? And right there, where that big, gnarly trunk splits wider than a caiman's tongue, can you see how all those leaves shelter the forest like the outstretched wing of a giant eagle? Have you ever seen anything so graceful and natural and...**_green_**?

Just feast your eye on all those different shades. Look how some greens are dark, like the thick moss on those tree trunks, but others are much brighter, like the shiny bellies of those leaves I was showing you earlier. Sometimes, when the sunlight pokes through in summer, this whole place glistens even brighter than the scales on Iggy the iguana's back. I really love the colour green – do you?

That's one of the reasons why it's so much better down here, beneath the leaves. Are you feeling this? There's no wind to ruffle my feathers or hot sun to burn my beak. I can laze beneath the shade of those cooling leaves without the rain turning me into a soggy potoo. You can tell that I belong down here, right?

Where do you come from, one-eye? I've never seen anything like you before. You've just got to tell me where you found that sparkly red spot. It's brighter than one of Rodrigo's tail feathers and I love the way it shines like a twinkly star at night. Maybe I should get one just like that for my beak. What do you think?

Hmm, you're still the silent type? That's OK,

one-eye. I understand. Sometimes, I wish more of my friends would take a leaf out of your tree. Just listen to them. Have you ever heard such a din? You're certainly a smart one – just like me. After all, what those sneaky predators can't hear, those sneaky predators can't eat, right? They live lower down and are too big and heavy to climb up here, so we all feel safe. That's why so many monkeys and snakes and birds and insects all make their own homes here, too, beneath the treetops. Between me and you, some days, it feels like a nest with too many chicks – barely enough room to swing a caterpillar. You know what I mean?

Hey, maybe if we perch here long enough, we'll bump into my buddy Fernando the frog. You'll love the colour of his skin – it's exactly the same as sunshine. Maybe I can introduce you to K-C, too. She's a kinkajou – so gentle and kind, furry and cuddly. She loves chewing on fat, juicy leaves. I prefer bugs. You probably do too, eh? But K-C says that if you don't eat green, you're just being mean.

So, one-eye, what are you looking at in the forest today, huh? Yesterday, it was colourful Rodrigo and

47

today... oh! I see, now. You're staring at Tolle, yes? You like sloths?

What am I saying? **Everyone** likes sloths. But you might be wasting your time, one-eye, if you're expecting Tolle to dance and move like Rodrigo. Tolle can't dance, see? Sloths like her don't do much showing off, either. They're much more like the branches of trees – they do everything really slowly, comprende? Tolle says that she just goes with the flow and she's 'in tune with the rhythm of the rainforest'.

Between me and you, one-eye, I don't always understand the things that Tolle says. The only forest rhythm that I hear is the screams of howler monkeys and the buzz-buzz of insects. Sometimes, I really wish that my poor ears didn't work, especially when I'm trying to get my afternoon siesta.

You know, you're lucky to catch me awake. I'm a night bird, really. Hunting yummy moths and insects is much easier when it's dark, and so is hiding from sharp-toothed predators like Jose the jaguar. But you're keeping me awake, one-eye. I need to figure out what you're doing here and tell my friends like Tolle the sloth.

Tolle says that we shouldn't worry. She thinks that I stress too much about the forest and those nasty tree-stealers.

"You can't stop the storm, Pedro," she tells me as she hangs lazily from her tree, "so better learn to dance in the rain, huh?"

What does she mean, one-eye? I already told you that sloths don't dance. I think that she teases me sometimes. She laughs at me when I tell her that

49

all this tree chopping is no joke but, hey, nobody will be laughing if all the trees get chopped down, right?

"Nothing is certain," she whispers with her eyes closed, "except for change itself."

Tolle is one of my best friends, one-eye, but sometimes that sloth can hurt a potoo's brain. Poor me! Poor me!

"But, Tolle," I say, "we've got to work together to save our home. Let's share to show that we C.A.R.E.!"

Tolle yawns, slowly turns away and says that it's already too late. She says that home is where the heart is, so we've just got to find a new place to love.

You tell me, one-eye – where will Tolle go? What new place is as safe as the forest for poor, steady sloths? Sometimes, it can take ages for her to climb a new tree, so how will she get anywhere fast enough? Tolle moves so slowly that she has green algae growing on her fur! She's turning the same colour as the tree leaves, one-eye!

50

Between you and Pedro, I think that Tolle just isn't thinking this through. She'd be way better joining the animals who C.A.R.E. and making a stand with us, right? That's why I told her that those nasty tree-stealers are the ones who should be leaving, not animals like us. It is not fair!

Do you know what she said?

"Life isn't fair, Pedro. Home is not a place; it is a peace that we must carry with us in our hearts."

What is she talking about? Does that make any sense to you? Tolle might be happy to move her home from tree to tree, but Pedro cannot do that! How could I leave my home behind? My favourite home in my favourite tree!

You should see it, one-eye — it is beautiful! I was hatched there and I have seen so many of my brothers and sisters fly from the safety of my tree's wide branches out into the rainforest. For me, it has been my favourite place to sit and rest for most of my life. Just wait until you see how tall it is, and the long, thick branches that are perfect for perching on. I can sit there for days, just watching the forest and seeing what my friends are doing. Trust me, it's the most wonderful spot in the whole rainforest.

In fact, you should be able to see it from here. Follow Pedro's wing! My tree is just over there... under these big leaves... past this tangle of branches and...

Whoa!

What?

Where has Pedro's tree gone? Where have **all** the trees gone?

My favourite tree should be right here, but now...

...there's just...

...nothing.

No, no, no! Poor me! Poor me! This cannot be happening, one-eye!

Those wicked tree-stealers have taken Pedro's special tree. It was my family tree, perfect for Pedro to share with his chicks, one day... and now it's gone, in the flap of a wing!

Poor me!

Still not talking, one-eye...?

Why so quiet? Why do you not care about Pedro and his special tree? I don't think that you're seeing how unfair this is, or how important every tree is! You need to see what things look like when too many trees have been chop-chopped, OK? So, I'll show you!

Come and see me tomorrow, but lower down, OK? Meet a friend of mine who nearly didn't survive when those nasty stealers cut down her favourite tree. I want you to see what's happening to poor animals like Winfrey. Maybe then you'll understand what unfair looks like.

Tomorrow, one-eye! Make sure you visit me tomorrow!

Poor tree. Poor me!

name: Daisy Field

class: 4JC

Rainforest Journal

8:19 a.m.

I know it's really early but mrs Curtis has given me and millie permission to use the computer during our breakfast club. mr Paterson had to open the computer room for us and he seemed a bit grumpy, but millie said not to worry because he's always like that before his nine o'clock cuppachino.

I asked her what a cuppachino was and she said it was some kind of yucky coffee drink, but mr Paterson drinks his from a mug, not a cup. maybe it should be called a muggachino. Neither of us knows why grown-ups like coffee — we both think that grown-ups can be a bit weird sometimes.

Guess what! I was right — mrs Curtis DID think I was silly to believe that the potoo knew that I was watching it. She reminded me that we're thousands of miles away and that those rainforest creatures don't even know what a webcam is, so there's no way that a bird like that would know that I could see it.

Even so, I told Millie about that potoo with the heart-shaped pattern, and how I'm starting to think that it might be watching me.

"You know, you could be like one of those attention-seekers that my mum sees at her salsa-dancing classes," Millie said. "They always think that people are looking at them, too."

"I'm NOT an attention-seeker. I'm sure that it was trying to show me something," I said.

Millie flicked her hair and said that I was probably imagining things again. Then, Jack Walters stuck his nose in and said that I'm always imagining things, such as imagining that I'll get a higher score than him in our next maths test. So I told him that at least I didn't think that a square root was some kind of horrible tree disease. Millie got quite cross with him and told him that it was rude to stick his tongue out like that.

I have to study the understorey today. Millie asked me if that meant we'd be looking for storybooks under the ground. When I'd finished giggling, I reminded her that the understorey is what we call the rainforest layer just beneath the canopy. Her cheeks went red and she said that she'd only been testing me, but I think that she'd forgotten what mrs Curtis had taught us.

"Why is it so dark?" she asked when I had logged on to the webcam.

At first, I thought that the lens might be dirty, but then I remembered that mrs Curtis had also told us that only a small percentage of the light from the emergent layer reaches this far down. That probably explains why looking through the lens was like looking through sunglasses.

We were supposed to be searching for that potoo but millie was way too interested in all the plants. She said that she recognised lots of them from her Auntie Clare's orangery (mum says that's just a posh name for a conservatory).

"Don't be silly, millie," I said to her. "Why would plants from the rainforest be growing in your Auntie Clare's house?"

But millie said that she was sure and even logged on to one of the other computers to prove it.

Well, it turns out that Millie wasn't being silly at all. I checked on the Internet again and she was right! Lots of those nice plants that we can buy at garden centres, like palms and ferns and bamboos and lots more, originally come from the rainforest. Wow — how amazing is that?! We've all probably got a piece of the rainforest in our homes. Double wow!

Mrs Curtis always says that time flies when you're having fun, and I think that we both must have been having a great time because the school morning bell sounded just as we had begun to count all the different butterflies that were fluttering past. We couldn't believe how many different types there were, or how beautiful they looked. We saw red ones, green ones, yellow ones, even multicoloured and patterned ones. A swarm of blue wings raced past the camera and the colour was so bright, it was like watching pieces of summer sky tumbling past.

Millie wants to come back at lunchtime to help me look for my dad's Bigfoot. She says that there's bound to be one there because the rainforest has been on earth for millions of years and if those Bigfeet live anywhere, it'll be there!

I didn't get to show millie the potoo, but I'm not surprised. I mean, what are the chances of seeing the same bird for a third time? It's probably off eating berries or catching moths or whatever potoos do. I doubt that I'll see it again.

CAM_03

UNDERSTOREY_CAM_03
WED_26/3_12:17PM

<<PREVIOUS   NEXT>>

Hey – why are you so quiet, one-eye? Can you see me? Perhaps it's too dark for you, down here. Sorry about that – the leaves and branches above us are so thick that the sunshine can't squeeze through. Maybe you're feeling like a sleepy sloth, huh? It always feels like night time to me in these parts, too, but don't worry that curious brain of yours – your one eye will still work fine down here, I promise. You know me, one-eye. I like the dark and my big eyes help me to see just fine – but there are lots of nasty predators lower down so keep your one eye peeled, OK?

Oh, how rude of me! I forgot to introduce you to my friend. This is Winfrey: an emerald tree boa. Can you see her beautiful, bright green scales? Isn't she lovely? When Tolle met Winfrey, she thought that my slithering friend was being rude and sticking her tongue out, but Winfrey uses that tongue of hers to taste the air; she doesn't know that it looks impolite.

This morning, Winfrey gave me some terrible news: she says that lots more trees were chopped down yesterday. That's right, more! Those nasty tree-stealers are getting closer and closer to Winfrey's home. This really worries me, one-eye. Think about it: what will happen to Winfrey and the rest of Pedro's forest friends when everyone's favourite trees are gone? What about Sonia the salamander, who loves living down here because all the humid air keeps her skin moist and soft? What are they supposed to do then – live in a hole in the ground like a burrowing worm? No, no, no!

You're **still** not talking to me. Is it something I've said?

Winfrey says that one of her big hugs might help to wake you up but I wouldn't recommend it, one-eye. I've told her to go easy, but Winfrey is a tree boa and she says that it's not her fault – she simply doesn't know her own strength! I'm sure that silly Winfrey thinks that a hug can solve almost any problem. She's such a softie. Do you know, last week, she even told me that she was thinking of becoming a vegetarian. I think that there's a better chance of a jaguar changing its spots – what about you? You should hear what she said to me yesterday!

"Pedro, we're worried about you. We think that you're getting way too sssssstressed by this tree-chopping isssssue." Winfrey curled that thick tail of hers around the trunk of her tree and flicked her forked tongue. "Your feathersssss are losing their shine and your beak looksssss like it might need an urgent tree-sssssap treatment."

Winfrey says that when she rubs against tree sap, it works wonders on her scales, making them glisten like river water in the sunlight. But I am a potoo on a mission; I don't need my beak to glisten. How would I be able to hide then, eh? Not to mention that the other potoos would laugh their feathers off at a shiny beak! No, thank you!

That's when Winfrey made her silliest suggestion. "You really should think about coming with usssss, Pedro," she hissed as she wound her long body around a branch and squeezed it tightly. "The treesssss aren't sssssafe for usssss any more — let'sssss find a new home, now."

Can you believe this, one-eye? That scaredy-snake thinks that I should actually consider joining the other animals who are leaving the forest. Phah! This potoo belongs in the rainforest. I'm the only one who seems to really C.A.R.E., one-eye! You remember C.A.R.E., right?

'Creatures Against Rainforest Evacuation'.

"Instead of leaving," I told Winfrey, "we should be working together to find a way to save the forest. We've got to dare to C.A.R.E., right?"

What do you think, one-eye?

One-eye?

name: Daisy Field

class: 4JC

Rainforest Journal

I'm sure that Jack Walters got most of his
spellings wrong on purpose, just so that Mrs Curtis
would make us do this week's test again. He
knew that I wanted to spend the whole of my
lunch break looking at the understorey webcam
— I don't care that he remembered how to spell
(embarassing) and I didn't.

Guess what, though! We actually saw that potoo
again — the one with the patterned chest! That's
got to be one of those (cow-incident) things that
Mum's always talking about. Like when you're
thinking about buying a new pair of red shoes
for dancing and then you see them in your
favourite charity shop window.

"Maybe all potoos have hearts on them," Millie
said to me. "It could be a different one each
time."

I showed Millie some pictures of other potoos on
the Internet and she soon changed her mind.

"Wait!" she said, putting her hand to her mouth.
"If we're seeing it every time we log on, that
means it's actually waiting around for us."

72

"That's what I've been trying to tell you! Why does nobody listen to me?"

"And that means..."

"...it knows that we're watching it." I finished the sentence for her.

"We should tell Mrs Curtis," Millie insisted, jumping out of her seat. "This could be REALLY important."

"We're not telling her yet." I tugged her back down onto the chair. "When I mentioned this yesterday, Mrs Curtis said that I was just being silly. We need more evidence."

For once, Millie agreed with me. After that, she couldn't take her eyes off the potoo. She said that she likes it, too, and that it looks like a startled owl chewing on an upside-down coat hook.

Could this bird really know that we are watching it? If only it could talk! Grandma Wilkins once had a friend who kept a cockatoo as a pet, and she says that it could talk the hind legs off a donkey. Millie says that her grandad once knew a dog in the army that could do morse code with its tail. millie's grandad says that the moon is made of cheese, though, so we don't always believe what he says.

DATSY

Whoa! You moved! Great! I guess my flapping wings really caught your attention, huh? Or was it my dashing potoo good looks?

Speaking of good looks, I've got to say how much I like that sparkling red spot of yours, and the way that it lights things up down here. It makes me think that I should ask a few fireflies to flash their bottoms to brighten up this part of the forest. Those clever bugs still won't tell me how they do that. I'd need a lightning strike to make my bottom glow like theirs.

Are you ready to see what those tree-stealers have done to the trees near poor Winfrey's home? Let's not waste another moment. Come quickly – follow your potoo friend.

That's right, turn your eye the same way that I flap my wing. See?

Hey, you're good at this. Now, look down!

Look... there... where Winfrey is showing you... can you see the light?

Instead of tall, elegant trees or a lush canopy,

the floor is covered with jagged wooden splinters and there is nothing but ripped, scorched, ugly stumps. Think of all the poor animals and creatures who have lost their homes, one-eye.

What's the point? Where's the sense in it all? Ah, Pedro just can't work it out.

Winfrey said that those horrible stealers dragged her trees away as if they were little twigs. Those trees had been in the forest for many seasons.

Winfrey's mama and papa coiled around those very branches when they were just snakelets. But then, **chop**! All gone in just a flap of a wing.

Winfrey is really worried now. She is so scared that the tip of her tail is twitching and tapping against the crumbly bark on our branch. She thinks that those tree-stealers might return here at any moment.

I try my best to reassure her.

"Look, Winfrey. You know what they say: lightning doesn't strike the same leaf twi-"

THUMP.

"Hey, Pedro..." Winfrey whimpers.

CRASH.

"...what'sssss that ssssssound?"

Did you hear that, one-eye? The dreadful sound below us of more trees falling – right now, in our forest! It's so loud, it sounds like the world is ending. What do we do?

"Let'ssss get out of here, Pedro!" Winfrey slithers as fast as her scales can carry her, towards the branch of the next tree. "It isn't sssssafe!"

Maybe I should fly away before I get chopped, too.

Wait! What am I **thinking**? This is my home!

"No,Winfrey! It's time to make a stand. It's time to show that we C.A.R.E.!"

"Sssssorry, Pedro. Thisssss is too big for a ssssssnake and a potoo. Sssssee you later." With a hiss, she disappears into a mass of green leaves.

Follow me, one-eye! Down to the forest floor! This could be your chance to see the tree-stealers with your own eyes – sorry, your own **eye**. Maybe you can think of a way to help Pedro stop it, huh?

Quick! Hurry, hurry – I really need your help!

name: Daisy Field

class: 4JC

Rainforest Journal

<u>12:40 p.m. (still Wednesday)</u>

At first, I thought that the potoo was having some
trouble with mosquitoes. Why else would it flap its
wings so much? That was when Millie pointed out
that it was only flapping one wing. It kept hopping
away from the webcam and back again, until I
used the keyboard to move the lens towards it.

"Do you think that he might be trying to
communicate with us?" Millie asked.

I was going to mention that the bird would be
wasting its time because neither of us can
understand French yet, so there's no way that
we'd be able to speak potoo. Then, Millie got
distracted – again!

"Look, there's a snake with it. Right there!
Perhaps they're friends, like us!"

I really don't like snakes, especially ones that look
as though they could wrap themselves all the
way around my bicycle! The potoo's friend was
pretty, though, and the lovely green and white
patterns covering its body helped it to blend in
with the leaves and branches. I think that the

snake must be a PREDATOR.

Camouflage allows animals to blend in with their **habitat** and hide from other animals. **Predators** sometimes use camouflage to avoid being detected by their **prey**.

I hope that it doesn't eat the potoo — that would be awful!

We looked at different snakes using the Internet search engine and it turns out that this snake is something called an emerald tree boa — 'emerald' tells us that it's mostly green, and 'tree' tells us... well, it lives in the trees, I guess. They don't have a poisonous bite like cobras and rattlesnakes, so they wrap themselves around other animals and squeeze them really hard.

Grandma Wilkins' hugs are really tight, especially when she hasn't seen me for a few weeks. I bet that the tree boa's hugs are even stronger than hers.

These non-venomous snakes kill their prey by constriction. The emerald tree boa holds its prey in its jaws and wraps its body around them, squeezing tightly.

Millie said that it looked like its skin had been freshly oiled — but since when did animals get beauty treatments in the rainforest? Millie does say some silly things...

12:46 p.m.

This is ANOTHER journal entry because I had to wait for Millie to fetch her inhaler from the classroom. She only took a few minutes and when she got back, we both used the cursor keys to follow the potoo when it hopped out of sight and then back again, until the webcam had turned as far as it could. I had to tell Millie not to touch the computer screen with her finger — Mr Paterson says that little fingers leave big smudges and he has to clean them with a special spray that's REALLY expensive.

"What's that, Daisy?" She hadn't listened to a word that I'd said, and jabbed a grubby finger towards the top corner of the webcam image.

The potoo seemed to be bouncing up and down, flapping one of its wings towards a gap in the trees that we could just about see in the distance. Where trees had once been, there were now only freshly cut stumps and the sunlight was pouring into the understorey.

We squinted at the pixelated image and saw something moving around on the edge of the sunlit area.

"What is it?" Millie squealed, before taking a few puffs on her inhaler.

"I think..." I replied, "...it might be the trees!"

You might not believe this, but some of the trees were actually MOVING! I don't mean that they were walking – trees don't have legs – but they were shaking, as if some kind of huge creature was wrestling with the bottom of the trunk. High above, the leaves rattled and shook and some even fluttered down to the ground. Millie snatched the mouse and turned up the volume as loud as it would go, and we leaned in close to the computer to listen.

An awful noise filled the computer suite and we both jumped in our chairs. It sounded like a monster was crunching on scrap metal somewhere very close by. As the webcam wobbled, a loud THUMP filled our ears and another tree trunk disappeared.

Something or someone was chopping the trees down. Sounds of sawing and hacking rattled through the speakers, and I reached over to turn the volume back down.

Millie looked horrified. "Is it your dad's Bigfoot creature?" she whispered.

Then, I explained to Millie all about the loggers that Mr Paterson had told me about.

"Daisy, I've just had the oddest thought." Millie grabbed my arm as if she was scared that I might run away. "What if that little potoo is trying to show us what those loggers are doing to the forest?"

I told you that millie sometimes says the silliest things. I mean, mrs Curtis is right — why would a potoo living thousands of miles away in the rainforest want to communicate with two schoolgirls in England?

Then again, it has been acting very strangely...

"What if it needs our help, Daisy?" Millie asked. "What if it's desperate?"

We both wanted to follow the bird. It kept flapping towards the forest floor and waving its wing again, and there's a webcam down there which might have shown us what was really happening. But right then, mrs Curtis stuck her head round the door and told us that we'd spent too much time on the computer already.

Neither of us had heard the bell ring for afternoon lessons, so I told her that we were sorry, then started to explain about the potoo and the loggers. But mrs Curtis used her loud voice to say, "That's all very well and good, but learning about the Romans is a more productive way to spend a Wednesday afternoon!"

millie whispered that it might be better if we
left the webcams alone until tomorrow morning.
She gets nervous when mrs Curtis uses her loud
voice.

I just hope that the potoo doesn't think that we
were ignoring it, or that we don't care about the
rainforest.

F-FLOOR_CAM_04
THU_27/3_08:03AM

<<PREVIOUS   NEXT>>

Oh, dear. I guess you're not quite as brave as your friend Pedro the potoo, huh? Did you get scared by the sound of the tree-stealers' chop-chopping, yesterday? Yes, that must be why you froze like a petrified tree stump. There I was, ready to take on the tree-stealers with my own bare wings, and you vanished! I spent so much time waiting for you that, by the time I was ready to face them alone, they had left. Such a pity – I really thought that we were a team, one-eye, but you seem even more frightened than Alice the agouti. Maybe that's why your red light isn't shining brightly at all today, huh? You're embarrassed.

If you **were** here, you could meet little Alice – she's the pretty little thing with the twitchy nose. My agouti friend lives down here on the forest floor. She likes it here. She says that there are always pools of lovely, fresh drinking water that fill up every time it rains.

Psst! Don't tell anybody, but sometimes, when Pedro is alone down here, your potoo friend checks his reflection in those water pools.

"D-don't get too close, Pedro!" Alice stammers. "What if caiman Camilla is staring back, huh?

Snap, *snap*!"

Alice tells me that there are lots of juicy insects and beetles to gobble up down here. "Yum, yum!" she squeaks, licking her paws.

Usually, I love bugs for lunch but I'm not so sure about the beetles that live way down here. Some are so ugly, I'm sure that they'd taste worse than a mouldy mushroom, or Felipe the frog's bright red skin. Eugh! Other bugs here are huge, with claws and wings and really tough shells. They might actually try to eat me!

Cast your one eye around this place. Can you think of living anywhere darker or damper? It's even gloomier than where Winfrey coils up for the night. And the awful smell of rotting leaves and sloppy mud – eugh!

Alice disagrees. "Pedro, this is the place to be! The conditions are j-just right for keeping my fur nice and warm. B-but could you squawk a little quieter, please?"

She glances anxiously over her shoulder as she speaks.

"Phah! I don't think it is the heat that is keeping you warm, Alice. This place is so full of nasty predators – I think that it must be all the running away that you are doing!"

You need to keep your wits about you down here, one-eye. If you were awake now instead of scared out of your tree, you'd be worried, too, that Jose the jaguar, with his fierce, biting fangs, could be waiting in one of those shadows. Or, just to the side of that green shrub – the one with leaves that look like long, droopy lizard's tongues – snappy caiman Camilla could be lying in wait with her sharp teeth and claws, wanting to make a quick snack of a nice, plump potoo like Pedro.

It's no wonder that poor little agoutis like Alice are always twitching and jumping and running away. Just the other day, I heard Annie the anaconda telling all her friends that she had made Alice jump so high that she bumped her head on a beehive! When I ask her why she doesn't jump up into the trees and live somewhere safer she just shakes her little head and tells me, "Nasties can't eat what nasties can't see!" She giggles nervously and darts under the nearest leaf.

Between you and me, one-eye, I think Alice would never live anywhere else – not without her favourite snack! She spends all her time sniffing out Brazil nuts and feasting on as many as she can get. It's all she ever thinks about, one-eye, and I think that she loves those nuts a little bit too much. She's nuts about nuts!

What I haven't told Alice is that these Brazil nut trees are one of the tallest of all the trees, reaching up and up and out the top of the canopy, where Rodrigo and his friends eat the biggest nuts before they fall to the ground. She wouldn't like it if she knew! She thinks that she's the only animal in the rainforest whose teeth can bite through the hard shells – but she hasn't thought about beaks, huh? I'll tell you what, though – I wouldn't like to be standing on the forest floor when those nuts drop from the canopy like little rocks.

Hey, one-eye, I really wish that you'd turn your fancy red light on today and start paying attention to your friend Pedro. We have work to do – we're on a mission, remember? Those nasty chopping tree-stealers could come back at any moment. They took more trees than Rodrigo has tail feathers yesterday and I worry that soon there'll be no trees left at all!

Poor me, poor me! Sometimes, it feels like only Pedro seems to C.A.R.E. Oh, and little Alice, of course – she says that she wants to C.A.R.E., too. In fact, I've been thinking that we should make her our next recruit. She keeps saying that if those tree-stealers try to cut down her beloved Brazil nut trees, she'll raise a vast agouti army to drive them away.

I like her determination, one-eye, I really do, but I'm not entirely sure if an agouti army would be quite enough to scare those tree-stealers.

"Pedro?" Alice is saying.

Pedro would much prefer a vast jaguar army, with fierce teeth and claws.

"Pedro…"

Imagine if Jose the jaguar brought all his friends to scare away the tree-stealers. Now, that would definitely –

"Pedro!"

Wait!

What is that? The growl of a fearsome predator?

Do you hear it? The grumbling?

It sounds close. Much louder than anything that I've heard before. Surely, it cannot be...

They're back, one-eye!

Look how the leaves tremble and quake! Look how the great trees thunder to the ground! Those tree-stealers must be really close!

"Nasties," says Alice. "Nasties coming!" She is collecting as many nuts as she can carry in her little paws.

Please, one-eye, turn your red light on. I need you to see this, and then we can figure out how to stop it – together!

Alice is leaving. "Hurry, Pedro!" she squeals. "Run!"

I should have known that little Alice doesn't C.A.R.E.

about anything but her Brazil nuts. How can we run away now, one-eye? This is what we've been waiting for! This is our chance to save the forest! I don't know what I'm going to do, but I know I have to do **something**!

Come on, one-eye. Do I have to tap you with my beak to make your light turn on? Please, wake up for your friend Pedro...!

name: Daisy Field

class: 4JC

Rainforest Journal

8:12 a.m.

I can't believe what has just happened. I didn't mean to scream, but I logged on to the forest floor webcam and guess what? I think that millie is right! That little potoo DOES know that we're watching him.

DOUBLE guess what? It's actually trying to TALK to me! That's why it was going tap-tappy-tap on the lens.

It wasn't alone. There was another little animal. It looked like a cross between a rat and a guinea pig, and it was REALLY skittish, like it was scared of its own shadow!

I didn't have time to study the animal because before I knew it, it had scampered away — and here's the part that you really won't believe. The potoo actually pushed the camera with its claw!

HONESTLY!

I used my arrow keys to move the camera left, but the potoo pushed it right.

Then, I pointed the lens up but the bird tugged it down.

All it would let me do was turn it as far to the right as I could. Then, I saw why...

...or at least I would have if Millie hadn't finally decided to turn up (late) and open her big mouth.

"Why's the screen so dark?"

"Shush!" I told her. But you know what she's like — she didn't shush at all.

"I can't see a thing. Hey, why's that bird trying to eat the camera?"

Only, it wasn't trying to eat the camera, was it?

"Wait!" Millie said, finally catching on. "Hey, I think it might be —"

That's when I shouted, "It's communicating!"

Millie muttered something that sounded like "...rude," but I didn't care. I was too busy chasing after the potoo.

We could see it hopping from place to place, away from the camera. It's REALLY crowded with trees and plants on the forest floor so I had to concentrate and zoom the webcam in and out. The camera has a red light on it, which was handy down there because it made it much easier to see as I operated it.

The little bird hopped first to the base of the closest tree, paused for a moment, and then peered around the wide trunk in the direction of a bright light which seemed to be burning through the forest floor. It was as if the sunlight was managing to shine right through the leaves and branches. We hadn't noticed it before because the camera lens had been pointing a different way, but it was so close that we could actually see what was in the clearing, especially when the potoo started to flap its wings like mad and hopped to the right so that I could zoom in on a spot between two smaller saplings.

That's when Millie jabbed her finger at the screen again and asked, "Are those men killing trees?"

The potoo was hovering in the corner of the

screen, so agitated that it was practically bouncing.

"Oh... that's awful," Millie stammered. I think that she might have started to cry. I don't blame her, though, because it really was awful. When I zoomed in as much as I could, we saw seven men with double-handled saws and huge axes and horrible, smoking chainsaws. They were hacking through giant tree trunks, as wide as sheds and cars, as easily as if they were lollipop sticks. Worst of all, each time a big tree fell over, the camera shook like we were in the middle of an earthquake.

That poor potoo must have been terrified. It kept looking right at the camera with those big, round, yellow eyes and shaking its head.

"Why is that bird still hanging around?" Millie asked me. "Does it want to get chopped?!"

"No," I told her, because I'd realised what was going on. It was like a little light had flicked on in my head. "I think it wants us to help."

Pedro will show you where to look, one-eye. Look at me, not Alice or all those runaway animals! This is it – the tree-stealers are here and it is our time to fight!

We need to get closer, one-eye, to face these nasty creatures and show them that they can't take **our** trees! Follow me!

Closer...

Closer...

What...

What IS it, one-eye?

Look at the size of it! Look how it towers like one

of the ancient trees that it so easily topples with one blow! How it chews through them with its fearsome teeth... and that sound! A roar like nothing Pedro has ever heard!

Quick, one-eye – hide!

How poor Pedro's feathers are trembling! Such strange creatures in our lovely forest, tearing down our precious trees... how can one potoo face all this on his own?

And yet... Pedro is the only one here.

Everyone in this forest can see them chopping and biting and stealing our trees, but nobody stops them.

Well, Pedro has had enough. It's time to put a stop to this. Let's show them how much we C.A.R.E. about our home, huh?

Look at us, though, one-eye: my tiny beak is not made for fighting, and you don't even have wings!

What could we possibly −

That's it! Alice's Brazil nuts! Those tough little shells are so hard, maybe they can hurt the tree-stealers as much as they hurt Pedro's head when they fall.

OK − I'm ready. Wish me luck, one-eye.

Potoo to the rescuuuuuuuuue!!!

DAISY

name: Daisy Field

class: 4JC

Rainforest Journal

<u>8:55 a.m.</u>

"Stop it! STOP IT!"

We both shouted at the tops of our voices but the loggers didn't stop. They couldn't hear us.

"They're killing the rainforest!" Millie yelled. "Why are they doing that? I thought that this area was supposed to be off-limits!"

I wasn't really listening to her. I was too busy watching that brave little potoo.

I could tell that the little bird wanted to do SOMETHING to stop the loggers. If it had been a bigger animal, it could have squashed those chainsaws and axes flat — but I guess there's not much you can do when you're only fourteen inches tall.

Still, it was a determined little thing. It used its claws to pick up nuts from the forest floor and throw them towards the loggers. When that didn't work, it flapped above the heads of the men who held chainsaws, dropping nuts from its beak like tiny bombs.

That didn't work, either. How could it? It was just one little bird against all those men and their sharp tools — but at least my potoo was trying. As I watched it getting more and more desperate, my eyes prickled with tears.

117

"It would take an army of birds to stop those loggers," Millie said.

"We need to do SOMETHING," I told her. "That bird trusted us enough to show us what was happening. We need to help it."

"How can we help a little bird from thousands of miles away?"

I didn't know the answer to Millie's question. I didn't know how to stop the men and I didn't know how to help. The only thing I knew was that I couldn't just abandon this poor little potoo, now that I could see how much danger its home was in. The rainforest is such an incredible place and these men were tearing it apart as though it were nothing.

Then, something really odd happened. Millie had a great idea.

"I know! Let's send an email to that famous David Battenburger. I bet he'd love to hear about the potoo. He might even make one of his television shows about it and help to stop those loggers before they chop down the entire rainforest."

"Good idea," I nodded. "Can we record this?"

Millie is much better with computers than I am, and found a way to save what we were seeing on the screen.

"This can be our evidence," I told her. "We can send this to David Battenburger."

"Mrs Curtis said that those people chop down twenty thousand square miles of forest each year," Millie continued. "No wonder that potoo is so upset. I think I'd be sad, too, if someone started chopping my home down."

The potoo was bouncing around on the forest floor between the legs of the awful men, making a racket louder than Millie's little brother did when he fell off the monkey bars. It pecked at the men's feet, flapping its wings frantically. The men began to kick out wildly at the hysterical bird with their huge boots and I started to panic that it would soon be stomped on.

Then, it was my turn to have a brilliant idea.

I snatched up the keyboard and began to hit

the buttons as quickly as I could — up, down, left, right, rolling the mouse wheel to zoom in and out at random.

"What on earth are you — ohh!" Millie gasped.

Thousands of miles away, in the depths of the rainforest, the little red light on the top of the charity's camera was flashing brightly as it moved up, down, left and right, and although we couldn't hear the sound of the camera lens zooming in and out, the loggers clearly could. Elbowing one of the other men, the largest logger began to look around until, at last, his eyes landed on our camera. He stopped kicking out at the potoo, looked right down the lens and began to stomp towards us!

Millie gasped and we both froze. I hadn't thought this far ahead.

We ducked beneath the computer table.

We both knew that the loggers couldn't really see us but, somehow, it felt safer on the computer room floor. All I could do was hope that my camera had distracted the men for long enough for the potoo to get away.

We sat there on the carpet for what felt like ages. After a while, Millie whispered that we should call the police and have those men arrested, but I don't think calling 999 reaches the police in Brazil. I had a better idea.

"Let's get Mrs Curtis. She always knows how to stop naughty people misbehaving."

name: Daisy Field

class: 4JC

Rainforest Journal

8:30 a.m.

See? I knew that Mrs Curtis would help us to figure out what to do. I remembered reading on that conservation charity's website that they work to stop illegal logging, so Mrs Curtis helped me to send them an email with a copy of our webcam video.

Well, guess what? It turns out that the conservation charity is really pleased with me and Millie. The lady who answered my email said that we should both get jobs as sleuths! I thought she meant sloths at first, but sleuth is actually another word for a detective — like Sherlock Holmes!

Anyway, it turns out that those horrible men who were chopping down those trees were illegal loggers. The lady explained that the Brazilian government awards something called a quota. These quotas give the good loggers permission to clear small parts of the forest but it also controls how much work they're allowed to do each year. This is how the rainforest is supposed to be protected.

Those naughty illegal loggers ignore this. They chop down as many trees as they like, in areas that the Brazilian government wants to protect and preserve and make off-limits. What nasty tree-stealers!

When the lady read my email and saw the video that I had sent (she said that it was really clever thinking), she called the authorities in Brazil and they rushed into the rainforest and stopped them. It's lucky, because the time in Brazil is three hours behind us in the UK and they were just waking up when we sent the email.

I haven't been back to the forest floor webcam yet to see if the men have gone. I hope that the little potoo is OK. I wish that there was a way to see it and tell it that we'd helped.

11:07 a.m.
How embarrassing! Ms Smeaton called me and Millie up to the front in our school assembly this morning and told everyone that we were heroes.

Millie loved it, of course. She even offered to sign autographs for the little children in the foundation classes. I think that my face has just about stopped glowing red. mr Paterson said that if my cheeks kept shining so brightly, he'd be able to rent me out to the coastguard as a replacement for the bulbs in one of their lighthouses. I don't think that mr Paterson is half as funny as he thinks he is.

ms Smeaton said that she was really proud of us and that we had done such a good thing, stopping those illegal loggers. She said that we might have saved a part of the rainforest where a new species of animal could be found, or even important medicines which might make it possible for doctors to save millions of people's lives in the future. millie asked her if we could get something called the 'No Bell Peas Prize' but I told them not to bother because I don't like peas – they make me come out in a nasty rash.

As a reward for being a rainforest hero, ms Smeaton said that I could take one last look at the webcams in the lesson before lunch. She also said that I can miss the whole lesson so that I can explore properly. Jack Walters isn't talking to me now. maybe he wanted to be a hero, too, or maybe he just wanted to miss our handwriting lesson.

That didn't matter to me. I didn't care about skipping lessons — I just wanted to get logged on and find my potoo. The last time I had seen it, big, dirty boots and axes had been aimed at it. I needed to know that it was safe.

I checked the forest floor first. It was even darker than before and it must have been raining above the canopy because water was dripping everywhere. I read that the canopy is so thick with leaves and branches that it takes the raindrops as long as ten minutes to reach the floor. For all I knew, it might have already stopped raining higher up.

The forest floor is my least favourite part of the rainforest. It's so gloomy and damp and brown! It's no wonder that so few animals live down here. I couldn't see the potoo anywhere. I did see its little friend, though — the one that looked like a cross between a guinea pig and a rat. It was chomping its way through one of the huge nuts that littered the floor.

Nearby, I also saw a long line of ants walking along one of the rotting tree trunks. We sometimes get ants in our kitchen during the

127

summer but these ants were nothing like ours —
they were massive. I definitely wouldn't want to
find those on mum's worktops!

The **agouti** (genus *Dasyprocta*) is a tropical
American <u>rodent</u> with a large head and body
but slender legs, small ears and a tiny, bald tail.
Agoutis are quite wary animals and are difficult
to see. They can move very quickly
when threatened and are able to jump up to
two metres off the ground.
They eat mainly fruits, nuts and seeds.

Habitat

I quickly did an Internet search.

I'm so glad that those ants were thousands of
miles away!

About
**Bullet ants get their name from the
shot of intense pain given by their
<u>venomous</u> sting. Victims may suffer
for up to 24 hours after being stung.**

As well as hunting for my potoo friend, I was also
desperate to see the area that millie and I had
saved. maybe there was already a family of

snakes moving back into their homes.
Perhaps the agoutis had already begun
to settle back in. Using the arrow keys,
I twisted the camera round before zooming in. I
wanted to see if what the lady from the charity
had said was true — that the loggers were really
gone — but I wasn't ready for what I saw.

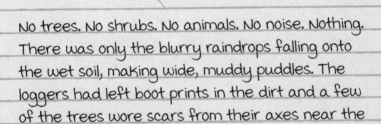

NOTHING.

No trees. No shrubs. No animals. No noise. Nothing.
There was only the blurry raindrops falling onto
the wet soil, making wide, muddy puddles. The
loggers had left boot prints in the dirt and a few
of the trees wore scars from their axes near the
bottom of their trunks.

My heart sank. We may have stopped the logging
from continuing, but we weren't quick enough to
save this part of the forest. I just hope that we
were quick enough to save the tiny potoo.

When I checked the webcam in the emergent
layer, it had stopped raining. In fact, the breeze
that always seems to be blowing up there had
chased all the clouds away and there was a
beautiful, blue sky. I think that the brightly

coloured macaws and lovely, blue cotingas were happy that the sun was shining because they were giddily soaring and rolling above the treetops like coloured tissues fluttering about in a breeze.

My potoo wasn't anywhere to be seen. I'd like to see it again, just to make sure that it's OK.

Where are you, potoo?

Daisy's Forest Floor Checklist

- [ ] Anacondas
- [ ] Jaguars
- [x] Insects
- [ ] New type of orchid
- [x] Potoo
- [x] (Agooty)

Hey, one-eye, can you hear that wonderful, delightful noise?

Listen!

Surely you can hear it now, right? I'm talking about the blissful sound of....

...absolutely **no chopping**!

Isn't it **amazing**? I can hardly keep still, I'm so excited!

Ah, I see your little red light is glowing brightly again, so I know that you're watching me. It's good to see you again – I've missed you!

I know what you're thinking: maybe your friend Pedro has been eating too many Brazil nuts, right? No, no, no, don't worry – Pedro hasn't gone nutty. Pedro is just a really happy potoo! No chop-chopping is good news for the rainforest. It means that the trees are staying right here, where they belong. It also means that Pedro's friends will all keep their homes, too. How great is that? That's what I call success.

I don't know what you did, one-eye, but it worked! I'm telling myself that you saw those nasty tree-stealers with your shiny, red one eye and you sent your friends to stop them. Hey, whether that's true or not, it makes Pedro feel good to think that we did this together. I just knew that you would C.A.R.E.! I can tell that you know how important it is to save the forest; you must love this special place as much as we do.

So Pedro wants to do something to thank you. Alice the agouti says 'thank you', too, and Winfrey the boa and Tolle the sloth. Even Rodrigo the show-off macaw sends his thanks, and I've already told you that Rodrigo is usually too in love with himself to think of anything but his pretty feathers, right?

Of course, they also say that Pedro did all the work. They say that without your favourite forest potoo, those chop-choppers would be free to destroy all our precious trees. Between me and you, one-eye, I quite like all the attention – and the free grubs that they keep bringing me, of course. Pedro the potoo is now a forest hero, but we both know that one-eye is a hero as well.

That's why I've decided that you deserve a little reward, too. At first, I thought that you might enjoy some big, plump, wriggly maggots, topped off with a juicy acai berry from one of my favourite trees. Those little gems taste like a rainbow exploding in your beak! Yum, yum! But then, I remembered that my good friend one-eye hasn't got a mouth or any claws – just that one big eye, huh?

I was discussing this with Tolle the sloth, who remembered that you like looking at pretty things like butterflies and macaw feathers and shiny leaves. So we put our heads together and thought that you might like to be the first to look at some nice colourful flowers, huh?

Haha! Sorry, your partner Pedro couldn't resist getting you a special something. Isn't this flower **amazing**?

Between me and you, I haven't seen one quite as pretty or patterned as this one anywhere in the forest before – and trust me, one-eye, Pedro has seen a lot of flowers. Maybe our three eyes are the first to ever see this, huh?

This is why I love living in this forest so much – you never know what amazing things you might find. Today, I found this pretty new flower – tomorrow, maybe a new bird or monkey or even a lizard! Next week, Tolle could find a tasty new fruit! Anything is possible in this magical place.

That's why it's so important that we all look after the forest and that we love and enjoy it together. I know that you agree, one-eye. All my friends have decided to stay, too, now that they know that the tree-stealers are gone. I'm so glad that we are all here together – it's our job to C.A.R.E. about the forest, because we all have to share the forest. Comprende?

name: Daisy Field

class: 4JC

Rainforest Journal

Just before the lunchtime bell rang, Millie came to
see what I was doing. I'm glad, too, because she
sat down just before I logged on to the webcams
for the final time, in the canopy.

I'd already taken a final look at the camera in
the understorey. In fact, I probably stayed too
long down there but I really love watching all
those amazing butterflies.

Grandma Wilkins is always saying how beautiful
flowers are, with so many colourful petals and
shades (mum says that her garden looks like
a painter has emptied all his paint pots across
her grass). I think that if she saw the rainforest
butterflies, even Grandma Wilkins
would admit that they're
the most beautiful things
on earth. Watching them,
it's as if someone has
chipped little flecks of colour
from a rainbow. Next time we do
painting or drawing with Mrs Curtis, I'm going
to paint my favourite butterfly: the black and
red one that looks like it's carrying an old man's
moustache on its back.

Millie says that she prefers bumblebees. Apparently, they help the planet more than butterflies, but butterflies make people happy so I told her that I'm not sure any job is more important than that.

We logged on to the canopy webcam so that Millie could see one of those sleepy sloths and I could keep on looking for my feathered friend. It took us a few minutes to spot the sloth but I didn't really care about it because, right there, sitting on one of the bigger branches, was my potoo. It's really well camouflaged in the trees but I'm getting pretty good at spotting it now. It was sitting quite patiently on a branch and looked healthy and happy. I breathed a HUGE sigh of relief and couldn't stop myself from grinning.

Millie laughed at me and said that we should probably have given it a name. She thinks that it looks like a Chuckie or an Eggbert, mainly because its eyes look like two egg yolks. My little potoo might seem a bit funny with its bulging eyes and squashed beak but it's really smart and, in its own quirky little way, it's quite cute, too.

mrs Curtis told me that this is the last time I'll be able to look at the webcams. Our password runs out today and it's another school's turn to use the webcams next week. Knowing that this would probably be the last time I'd ever see my potoo friend made me feel quite sad, but I told Millie that I had a cold when she asked me why I was sniffing. I'm sure that she was too interested in watching that sloth hang from its branch to notice me wiping tears from my cheek.

I wondered why the potoo was still hanging around the webcam, even after the loggers had left the forest. It didn't seem agitated or worried any more but it was still staring directly into the lens and chirping away. I even thought that I saw it wink at me, but I didn't tell Millie because she would have said he just had some dust in its eye or that I was imagining things again.

As I watched, searching the screen for anything new to write about before I had to log off for good, my potoo began to bounce around on its branch. It still seemed to be gabbling away and, as it hopped to the side and lifted one wing, I saw what it had been hiding.

I gasped.

Millie jumped. "What?!"

The most wonderful orchid — even more beautiful than any in Grandma Wilkins' collection or in any picture — was growing on the branch beside my potoo. Five petals, each the shape of a teardrop, stretched outwards from the centre. Every one was splashed with an identical pattern of purples, blues, yellows and oranges, and it was truly the most stunning flower that I have ever seen.

We checked the Internet for pictures of other orchids and we couldn't find one that looked as colourful or as beautiful as the potoo's. Millie said that we should send a screenshot to the conservation charity to see if it's a brand new flower. We might even get to name it for Grandma Wilkins!

Even though I was excited by the orchid and seeing my potoo, I had discovered something even more important than either of them. There are probably hundreds or thousands of brand-new orchids and insects and animals hidden away in the middle of the rainforest — including Dad's

Bigfoot — and I think that's what matters most.

When mrs Curtis asks me what I've learned from my observations, I'm going to tell her that we've got to look after the rainforest more, so that we can protect all the amazing things that grow and live there. After all, the rainforests have been around for over fifty million years now, and our job should be to make sure that they're here for another fifty million years, too.

I wonder if that's what the potoo has been trying to tell me all along...

Daisy's Tips for Helping the Rainforest

Every single person can help the rainforest in lots of ways just by making some small changes. Here are the things that I am going to do to help:

1. I'm going to look out for symbols on foods like coffee, chocolate and tea that show which products are certified by rainforest charities. This means that the products are definitely grown in a sustainable way.

2. Some companies make paper that is environmentally friendly. I'm going to ask my headteacher, Ms Smeaton, if our school can buy our copy paper from one of those.

3. I want to raise funds to donate to an organisation that works to conserve rainforests. I could hold a bake sale, sell some of my old toys or even hold a school fundraiser!

4. Palm oil is a type of vegetable oil that comes from oil palm trees. You can find palm oil in some brands of chocolate, shampoo, lipstick, margarine and soap, just to name a few products! Sometimes, to make way for oil palm plantations,

huge areas of rainforests are cut or burned down. When this happens, local people lose their homes and amazing species are put in danger. I'm going to ask mum if we can stop buying so many products which use palm oil, to help to stop this from happening. When we go out shopping, I'll look for labels showing that products don't contain palm oil or that any palm oil in them has been grown sustainably.

5. I want to learn even more about what parts of my daily life rely on tropical forests so that I can appreciate them even more.

How much can you remember about the story? Take this quiz to find out!

1. Who or what is 'one-eye'?

2. What does Pedro call the people who are chopping down the rainforest?

3. What does C.A.R.E. stand for?

4. What kind of flower does Pedro show to the camera at the end of the story?

Answers: 1. the webcam 2. tree-stealers 3. Creatures Against Rainforest Evacuation 4. an orchid

Challenge

Look at the illustration of the rainforest and its animals.

The names of some of the animals have been scrambled.

Can you work out what they are?

1. gjuaar
2. artnaluat
3. ancout
4. macian
5. otoop

Scan the QR code to see a colour version of this picture and a full list of the animals featured.

Discussion Time

? How does Daisy feel about taking part in this project? What evidence can you find that supports this?

? Why do you think the book contains both extracts from Daisy's diary and webcam footage from the point of view of Pedro?

? Why do you think it's important to learn about the rainforest?

? Do you think that any logging should be allowed in the rainforest? Why or why not?

Discover more from Twinkl Originals...

Continue the learning! Explore the library of Rainforest Calling activities, games and classroom resources at twinkl.com/originals

agouti

butterfly

Scarlet Macaw

Brazil nuts

llet ants

Fruits and Vegetables

Welcome to the world of Twinkl Originals!

Board books
Ages 0-3

Picture books
Ages 3-7

Longer stories
Ages 7-11

Books delivered to your door

Enjoy original works of fiction in beautiful printed form, delivered to you each half term and yours to keep!

1 **Join the club** at **twinkl.com/book-club**

2 Sign up to our **Ultimate membership**.

3 **Make your selection** – we'll take care of the rest!

The Twinkl Originals app

Now, you can read Twinkl Originals stories on the move! Enjoy a broad library of Twinkl Originals eBooks, fully accessible offline.

Search '**Twinkl Originals**' in the App Store or on Google Play.

ook out for the next book club delivery

A TWINKL ORIGINAL

twinkl

ENZO'S EGG

Coming February 2022

When Enzo faces a tough time in his life, he retreats to his egg. The people who love Enzo want to help – but can anyone understand what he really needs? How can you open an egg without cracking it?

This gentle story uses metaphor to address difficulties around loss and mental health.

Can't wait?
Get the digital version at
twinkl.com/originals